Tap Out

Sean Rodman

orca soundings

ORCA BOOK PUBLISHERS

Library and Archives Canada Cataloguing in Publication

Rodman, Sean, 1972–, author
Tap out / Sean Rodman.

(Orca soundings)
Issued in print and electronic formats.
ISBN 978-1-4598-0875-1 (pbk.).— ISBN 978-1-4598-0876-8 (pdf).—
ISBN 978-1-4598-0877-5 (epub)

I. Title. II. Series: Orca soundings
PS8635.O355T36 2015   jC813'.6   C2014-906685-6
C2014-906686-4

First published in the United States, 2015
Library of Congress Control Number: 2014952067

Summary: Darwin is unstoppable in the illegal fight club.
But what is he fighting for?

MIX
Paper from
responsible sources
FSC® C016245
www.fsc.org

*Orca Book Publishers is dedicated to preserving the environment and has
printed this book on Forest Stewardship Council® certified paper.*

Orca Book Publishers gratefully acknowledges the support for its publishing
programs provided by the following agencies: the Government of Canada through
the Canada Book Fund and the Canada Council for the Arts,
and the Province of British Columbia through the BC Arts Council
and the Book Publishing Tax Credit.

Cover image by Getty Images

ORCA BOOK PUBLISHERS
PO Box 5626, Stn. B
Victoria, BC Canada
V8R 6S4

ORCA BOOK PUBLISHERS
PO Box 468
Custer, WA USA
98240-0468

www.orcabook.com
Printed and bound in Canada.

18 17 16 15 • 4 3 2 1

Chapter One

Dear Son,

It has been a while since I wrote to you. I am sorry and will not make excuses for that. The last letter you sent to me was about how much you hate your new school. I think that I would hate it too, but your mother thinks it is the best for you.

And there is not much I can do from where I am, is there?

So all I can do is give you some good advice. I think it is a father's job to tell you how the world is. Not what it should be. And I tell you that you must fight every single day of your life. Whether with your fists or just the way you live every day, you will have to fight for everything. I know that I have.

And so when you wrote that you hate your new school, that is okay. In fact, I think hate is good.

Because in the end, the winner of any fight is decided by a few small things.

The winner is the one who doesn't crap his pants.

The winner takes fewer punches than the other guy.

And the winner hates just a little bit more. And has enough control to let that hate out, hit by hit.

Dad

Chapter Two

"I don't want any trouble," I say.

It's a lie.

I'm actually kind of hoping the bald guy makes the first move. It's been one of my bad days, where my skin doesn't feel like it fits. Like I'm just waiting for someone to come at me. I'm edgy. Pissed off. Looking for a fight. And I found one—this over-muscled chrome dome shoving around a skinny kid with glasses in front of the convenience store.

The bald guy in the Lakers jersey looks slowly over his shoulder at me and then snorts. He exaggerates letting go of his victim—his fingers snap open to release the kid with glasses. The kid's wearing the same uniform as me. The uniform of Norfolk Academy.

Bald guy swaggers toward me. "What, you standing up for him? Private-school code of honor?" He laughs and shakes his head. "Would be funny, except your friend Jonathan here owes me money. So, you step off and let me finish my business."

"Mason," says the victim—Jonathan—from behind him. "Take it easy, bro. We can sort—"

I stand my ground. "Know what? I don't know him and I don't know you. And I don't care what your business is with him. But you don't do it on the street in front of me."

"Or what? You gonna get your nice white shirt all dirty?" Mason gives me a shove, both hands on my chest. I stumble and then come back fast. Push him with one hand on his Lakers jersey. He doesn't move, but his expression darkens. Game on.

We circle, staying on the balls of our feet, staying light. Mason fakes a punch, just testing me out. I keep out of range. He starts to get frustrated and holds his hands out, as if to say, "What are you waiting for?"

I fall for it and step in toward him with a wild roundhouse swing. I miss, and he takes the opportunity. A hard jab connects with my jaw. I stagger back, falling to my knees. Little zips of light flash in my eyes.

Mason laughs. He turns to his victim, who is still pressed against the front of the convenience store, eyes wide. "Jonathan, you need a better bodyguard." While he's turned sideways, I push up off from the ground and wrap both of my arms around Mason's legs. He goes down like a tree, grunting as he hits the concrete. Then I'm on top of him, one forearm across his throat, pressing hard.

"Are we done?" I growl. He grimaces, shakes his head. His eyelids are starting to flutter. Another couple seconds and he'll be out. But a firm hand grabs my shoulder and pulls me backward, off of him.

"What the hell are you kids doing?" It's the owner of the convenience store behind us. A short guy with a white mustache and a pissed-off expression. Mason is coughing on the ground. "Look, I don't want any trouble. All of you, get out here before I have to call the cops!"

"Hey, no cops. There's no problem," says Jonathan, stepping forward and pulling me away from the irate owner. "Let's go." He pushes me down the street, away from the store. I look back and see Mason, still on his hands and knees. Head down and breathing hard.

"I think I owe you," says Jonathan. He keeps us moving down the sidewalk, then across an intersection on the red light. "Who are you?"

"I'm Darwin—Dar," I say. "You don't owe me. I just didn't think he should push you around."

"Yeah, well. You certainly know how to push back," says Jonathan.

I rub my jaw, still sore from that big hit. Trying to figure this guy out. Jonathan is a thin kid, his uniform hanging off him like it's half a size too big. I've seen him around before but honestly never taken much notice. He's clearly not one of the really popular kids, but instead moves between the various cliques of the school—jocks to nerds—without a problem. Everybody tolerates him. Not sure if anybody really likes him though.

We hustle alongside a low brick wall, then left through a big black gate. The words *Norfolk Academy* scroll in an ornate iron arch over the gate. Back to school. I try to brush some of the dirt off my jacket. Touch my face to see if there's any blood.

Jonathan stops me just before we enter the big main building. He straightens his glasses and then squints at me. "Doesn't matter what you say. I still owe you one, all right? And I think I know how to pay it back."

Chapter Three

Jonathan finds me the next day in the cafeteria. The big hall is filled with rows of students eating. The clattering of plates, cutlery and teenage chatter is loud. I drown it out with my iPod. Ever since I arrived a month ago, I eat alone anyway. The tunes keep me company.

But today I'm not alone. Jonathan drops onto the bench across from me, smacking his cafeteria tray onto the table.

"Hello, Downtown Darwin Stone." He holds a hand out for a fist bump. I just look at it and slowly pull my earbuds out.

"What did you call me?" I say. "Downtown?"

"Yeah, because you're from the inner city, right?" He pulls his hand back. "That's all anyone knows about you, actually. That you transferred from a public school downtown."

I nod and pay attention to finishing off my sandwich. Jonathan watches me for a moment, still half smiling. Then he starts into his own lunch, speaking around a mouthful of lasagna.

"They also say you came here because you decked a teacher at your last school. Based on what you did to Mason yesterday, I'd say that sounds about right." Jonathan's forkful of lasagna stops midway to his mouth. "Is it true?"

I sigh and rub the bridge of my nose. "No, it's not true. I got in a couple of fights. But so did everybody else. It's just a fact of life."

Jonathan pushes the orange-red pasta around his plate. "So why did you come to Norfolk?"

Because my mom wanted me to have some "good influences" in my life. Not to end up in prison like my dad. Or bleeding out from a random drive-by shooting.

"I was too smart for my last school," I say. "Norfolk couldn't resist me."

"Right." Jonathan snorts, nearly spilling the milk he's drinking. He finishes with his food and pushes the tray away.

"Okay, smart guy. Remember how I said I could pay you back?"

"Yeah."

Jonathan leans over the table and motions for me to come closer.

"I run a fight club, and I want you to be in it."

"A what?"

"A fight club. Bunch of guys get together and take each other on. Man to man. No holds barred. The audience pays me, I take bets on the winner. That kind of thing." His smile is wide and white, like his dentist did something extra to make it shine.

"Sounds kind of stupid," I say. "And illegal."

"Yeah, it's both," Jonathan says. "But I've had two fights so far, and it's made a crapload of cash. You could make a lot of money."

I cross my arms. "What do I have to do?"

"I want you to be my next star," he says. "My fighter. I'll pay you to be in the ring."

I watch him closely. "Why me?"

"Because I've seen you in action." The smile goes to a thousand watts. "And you're a natural."

Chapter Four

Jonathan was right. I am a natural. Two fights in, two rich kids are on the floor.

Now for number three.

"Listen to that crowd," says Jonathan. "They can't wait to see you in action again, amigo. You're a freakin' rock star."

I nod, not really hearing him, getting into my zone. I slip the mouthguard in and wiggle my jaw until it's locked in place. I flex my hands, roll my head around, bounce on my toes. Trying to get loose, to breathe steady.

Across the circle the crowd has left open, my opponent is taking his gray blazer and white dress shirt off.

Seriously?

He shouldn't do that. What might have been muscle hidden under the shirt is revealed as pasty-white flab, scattered with some curly red pube-like hair. He's bigger than I am, way bigger. But I think size is all he's got.

I look around for Jonathan, but he's back in the crowd. Working them, getting bets lined up. I don't know how much he makes for organizing these things, but I'm getting fifty bucks a fight. He must be making more than that, what with maybe twenty guys paying admission and laying bets. But they can afford it.

For a moment I let myself scan their faces. Most seem to be around my age, sixteen, seventeen years old. Wearing all the same brands. Shoes that cost more than my mom pays in rent. Feeling all grown up because they're slumming it at Jonathan's illegal fight club. Makes me sick. Where I grew up, you fought because you had to—big fish trying to eat the little fish. These guys are watching this fight like it's something on an Xbox. Entertainment.

But it pays.

"Stretch it out, lots of drama. Okay?" Jonathan's back, shouting in my ear. "Just like last time?"

I nod. Jonathan slips on his sunglasses—ridiculous, since we're inside a dimly lit garage. Then he walks into the middle of the empty space the crowd is gathered around. He holds up his arms for silence.

The roar descends to a murmur.

"Ladies and gentleman, boys and girls."

Jonathan likes his moment.

The light flashes off his sunglasses, and his lips sneer back from perfect teeth. "Welcome to the Norfolk Academy fight club!"

A roar.

"You all know the rules, right?"

Laughter.

"First rule, there is no fight club. That means put your phones away. What you see here stays here." He puts a finger to his lips as he turns around, clowning it up for the audience. "Now the main event. In this corner, senior at Norfolk Academy, halfback on the football team, the heavy hitter himself, Savage Sam Tilson!"

Sam stands up across from me and turns in a circle, beady eyes trying to look fierce but only looking piglike. The crowd chants his name anyway.

"And in this corner, a new arrival at Norfolk but already making a name for himself, Downtown Dar Stone!"

I get up off the broken office chair I've been sitting on and stare at the crowd. The way they shout, I'm pretty sure most of them are looking forward to watching the crap get beaten out of me.

"All right, gents." Jonathan motions for the two of us to approach him in the center of the ring. Actually, *ring* makes it sound formal. The whole space is just an empty garage with blacked-out windows, lit by hanging lightbulbs that throw crazy shadows around. When we first arrived, it smelled faintly of wet concrete and oil. Now that stench is overlaid with a haze of teenage sweat and body spray.

"Gents, I'd say keep it clean—but I know you won't." Jonathan gets us to tap our fists together, then dances back out of the way.

I circle Sam with quick little steps, hands up around eye level. Sam kicks out at me, a flashy high thing. Some sort of martial-arts movie must be running through his head. I easily step away from it and swat at his leg as it goes by. That throws him off balance, and I rush him. A quick right hook at the mouth. Sam turns his head to miss it. I follow with a straight jab that connects with his ear. But now I'm too close, too open.

I back up fast. Not fast enough. Sam gets a solid couple of hits to my stomach on my way out. Hurts. We circle around each other. Blood dripping from the side of his face. Me bent over a little from the pain.

"What, you scared?" says Sam. "Should be. Get back to the estates where you belong."

I see Jonathan over his shoulder, stopping a pretty girl from taking pictures with her phone. Distracted, I don't see Sam coming until it's too late. Lucky for me, he has crappy aim. His fist smacks near my forehead, probably hurting him more than me. But the surprise gives me a shot of adrenaline, and I fly at him. A jab to his face to throw him off balance. Then I grab his right shoulder with both hands and bring him down hard. Straight into my knee as I drive it up into his solar plexus.

The air whooshes out of him. When I let go, he drops to the concrete floor, gasping for breath. I fall on top of him, pinning his neck with my left hand, his chest with my knee. I raise my right fist, cocked back and ready to smash down on his face.

"Your turn to be scared," I say. "Are we done now?"

Sam's beady eyes bore defiantly into mine. He brings one arm up to try to push me off. I ignore it and tighten my grip on his neck.

"One more chance. Tap out?" I say.

Chapter Five

His face goes redder than before, almost shading into purple. He grimaces, then smacks the floor twice with his hand. I stand up and back away. Sam doesn't bother getting up, just lies there wheezing.

"We have a winner!" says Jonathan, walking back into the middle of the ring and holding up one of my arms.

He's got his big, wide toothy smile on. When he turns away from the crowd toward me, I can tell from his eyes that he's actually pissed.

"What the hell was that?" he hisses. "That lasted, like, ninety seconds? Dar, these people paid money for a movie, and you gave them a commercial." He drops my hand, shakes his head and walks back to his friends in the crowd. Sam is still lying on the floor. I lean over and offer him a hand up.

"Screw you," he says, rolling away.

As he struggles to his feet, I snap my leg out and flick one leg from under him. He collapses to the floor again with the sound of a bag of dirt hitting the ground.

Someone grabs me from behind. "What the hell?" It's one of Sam's buddies from the football team. He's not alone. Should've controlled my temper. That was stupid. But before it can get out of hand, Jonathan appears at my side.

"Hey, hey, hey. Let's keep the fights in the ring, all right? Take it easy. Dar, you apologize for that." I look over at Sam, who is all smiles now that he's leaning on two football buddies. Big man now that I'm outnumbered. But Jonathan's right. I nod.

"My bad. I'm sorry." I extend my hand to Sam a second time. And again he doesn't take it. He spits on the ground. Laughs.

But this time I keep my cool. Watch them walk away, joining the rest of the crowd heading for the exit.

"Listen, Dar," says Jonathan, turning me toward him. "You have got to do better next time. That was ridiculous."

"What?"

"The world's fastest fight, followed by…that?" He gestures at Sam and his teammates. "You're going to be on their hit list for weeks. Worse, I might even get on that list if you keep it up."

"Yeah, you got my back, don't you?"

"Dar," he says. "This isn't about our business partnership."

I rub one hand over the lump on my head. My mouth tastes like copper. "Then I don't think this partnership is going to work." I pull on my hoodie.

"Ah, don't get like that." Jonathan rolls his eyes and puts a hand on my shoulder. I shrug it off. "I'm saying that you and I, we've got a good thing going. You're the star of the fight club. And I'm making us money."

I stare at him for moment.

"You're a shark, man," Jonathan continues. "I'm like those fish that hang out with sharks, clean them up, show them where the food is."

He slaps a bunch of bills into my hand. I flip through them. Fifty, as promised. "So don't screw up this relationship, all right?"

I stuff the money into my jeans pocket, grab my backpack and head for the door.

"What, you've got nothing else to say to me?" says Jonathan.

I turn back. "What do you mean?"

"Not even a thank-you? For the money? For keeping Sam's crew from kicking your ass?"

I just mumble, "Thanks" and pound the door open to the bright sunshine.

The empty garage is a few blocks from the grounds of Norfolk Academy. About ten minutes if I hustle. And afternoon class starts in fifteen. Jonathan originally wanted the fight club to be at night, because it would be cooler. But it turned out lunchtime brought in more of a crowd. So that's when we fight.

I pull on my blazer as I cut across the grassy quad. The temperature drops as I pass underneath the big old oaks.

I'm almost to the rear entrance of the McAlister Building when I see her. Keisha is walking in from the other direction, hands dancing around as she tells a story to her friend. Crap. I don't think I look too roughed up from the fight. But I don't want her to ask questions I can't answer.

I angle toward the other side of the building. I've almost made it when I hear her call out.

"Dar!" She's waving at me, big smile. Her friend looks less impressed, binder clutched to her chest.

I nod at her, hesitate for a second and then walk over.

"Keisha. I didn't see you—"

"It's okay. Where you coming from?" she asks.

For a minute I think she knows where I've been. Then I look at her brown eyes, wide and trusting. Tough to lie to. But she doesn't know about the fights.

"Just getting something for lunch. You know, at the Quik Mart."

"What happened to your forehead?" says her friend, raising an eyebrow. "It looks like—"

I cut her off in a rush of words. "It's fine. Gym class. So hey, Keisha—you still up to going out tomorrow?"

Keisha nods, her smile turning a little shy. "Yeah, of course. Pick me up at seven." She turns, brown hair cascading back over her shoulder just like in the shampoo commercials. For the hundredth time I wonder what I'm thinking, trying to hang with her.

Her friend stares a minute longer at me, then hustles to catch up to Keisha.

Chapter Six

By the time classes finish, I'm wiped. I doze off on the subway ride home, head against the glass. Wake up with a start right before my stop, wondering for a second where I am. The walk to Franklin Estates wakes me up a little, the cold fall air making my lungs ache. Crossing the quad to our apartment tower, I see a couple of kids playing basketball in the parking lot. TB waves to me from his usual post, slouched in a beat-up lawn chair outside his townhouse. I don't wave back—I just hurry into the lobby of my building.

The elevator smells like cat piss. The old lady riding in the elevator with me has her nose wrinkled up and her eyes locked on the changing numbers above the door. Like she can make me and the tangy stench go away, just like that. When we get to her floor, I hold the door open for her. She doesn't thank me, just shuffles out. Never meets my eyes. I could get mad, but it happens every day. Kid with big muscles, mean face, hoodie, jeans. I fit the profile.

When I get to the apartment, I realize I've forgotten my key again. I bang on the door until I hear the rattle of the dead bolts on the other side. The door swings wide open, and there's my little brother staring at me with big eyes.

"Runt, dammit. What I'd tell you?" I say.

"About what?" he says, knowing he screwed up but not how.

"You always use the chain. Never throw the door open like that." Not that the little chain would stop some of the real predators around here. But the boy needs to at least try.

"Sorry, Dar," he says quietly.

"Good little man," I say, wrapping my palm over his head and giving it a little shake. "Where's Mom?" He nods toward the kitchen. Our apartment is small, but bigger than some in the building. Two bedrooms. Runt and me in one, Mom in the other. Kitchen opening into a living room with a red couch we got from the thrift store and hauled up in the freight elevator. A small table for eating. Mom's tried to make it cheerful with some posters she found at a garage sale—pictures of sand and palm trees, happy people spending money.

I drop my backpack on the hallway floor and stick my head around the corner.

"Dar!" says Mom, her head surrounded by a cloud of steam. She finishes draining a pot of pasta and clangs it back on the stove. "You're just in time to wash up for dinner." I nod and muscle into the bathroom beside Runt. Make him wash his hands right. By the time we get back, Mom has put two bowls mounded with noodles and sauce on the table. She pulls off her apron, and I see she's wearing her uniform.

"Sorry, guys. I'm going to have to run to the drugstore. Judy called in sick, so I've got an extra shift." She leans in to give Runt a kiss, then over to me. "Dar, you make sure the dishes get cleaned right—" She stops short, staring at the purple bruise on my forehead. "Explain what happened. Right now."

"Aw, Mom. It's nothing. Gym class. Basketball. I smacked into someone. I was watching the ball, not where I was going."

She tenderly pushes back my short hair. Testing the bruise with her cool fingers.

"What did the nurse say?"

"The school nurse?" Is Mom testing my story? "Never saw her. The teacher didn't think I needed to." I push her hand gently away. "Seriously, no big deal."

She drills into me with her eyes.

"You know I sent you to that school to get you away from the rough stuff, right?"

I nod.

"But you've got to make it work. I find out you're fighting again, even if it's on the basketball court, I'll—" She stops and shakes her head. I bet she doesn't know what she'll do, because there aren't a lot of options left.

I stare down at the noodles, cooling in their bowl.

"I get it, mom," I say. "This was just an accident, okay?"

She sighs, then checks her watch. "I've got to run. We'll talk about this later." She shrugs on her coat and trades her slippers for work shoes.

"Do what I said. Clean up. Get your homework done. Riley's got some math—"

"I'll take care of it, Mom. I will."

She opens the door, then looks back at me. "I know you will, Dar."

Runt is pretty good for the rest of the evening. He works hard, scrubbing down the counters while I wash the dishes. I swear the boy doesn't have an Off switch—he talks nonstop, and I just have to pretend like he's a radio or something. Tune him out. We get his homework done, and then I let him watch TV in his pajamas. I sit at the table and work on my essay. History. The start of World War I, assassinations, terrorists. We were assigned a country to write about, and I was given Switzerland. I didn't even know where it was at first, but it's actually kind of interesting. I'm on a roll with the writing when Runt suddenly speaks up.

"I just saw Dad on the news," he says, still watching the glowing screen in the corner of the living room.

"What?" I stand up from the table and go over to the couch. It's the eleven o'clock news—already? How'd that happen?—and it's a clip about Newhaven Penitentiary. "You did not see him."

"They showed a bunch of guys in the courtyard, and he was right there."

I sit down, pushing him over to make a little room. But the clip is over, and now they're talking about the weather.

"It's a big place, Runt. And those guys all look the same in the blue jumpsuits."

"No, I know it was him!" he says. "It was!"

"All right, okay." I hold up my hands. "Don't cry about it. It was him. Fine." We both watch the weather map, full of colors and lines. Rain tomorrow, getting colder.

"How'd he look?" I ask.

"Well, he was in the background," Runt says, looking up at me uncertainly. "But I think he looked proud."

"Proud?" I say. "What do you mean, proud?"

"You know that look he had when I drew something nice and he'd put it on the fridge? Like that. Proud."

I study Runt's smooth face in the blue light of the television, watching to see if Dad appears again. Then I reach out and pull his little body close to me.

35

"Damn straight he's proud. Proud of his two men, right?"

Runt looks up at me seriously. "You shouldn't swear, Dar."

I just laugh. "Time for bed, Runt. Too much TV is gonna rot your mind."

Chapter Seven

I hear Mom rattling the locks on the door and squint at the blinds beside my bed. Dim gray light from outside, so it must be before six. I put on some clothes, trying not to wake Runt. By the time I get to the kitchen, Mom's got the coffee-maker going.

"How'd it go last night?" she whispers to me.

"It was good. Got my essay done. Runt behaved himself."

"Riley," she corrects me without thinking about it. "Call him Riley."

I shrug and help myself to coffee and toast. I start eating over the sink and hear Mom sigh. "Sorry. I'll get a plate," I say.

"It's not that. But, yeah, get a plate."

I grab a chipped one from the cupboard and turn to face her. She's slumped against the fridge, mug in hand. All of a sudden I notice how old she looks, how tired. It's funny how she changes. Some days she acts young, which is the truth—she's only in her early thirties. But some days she's a hundred years old, like right now. Makeup not hiding the wrinkles, the worry. Not that I'd ever say that to her.

"Rough night at work?" I ask.

"Not too many crazies." The all-night drugstore she works at tends to attract the weirdo 2:00 AM crowd. "I was glad for the extra shift." She looks up uncertainly from her mug at me. "We need the money."

"Always." I wipe crumbs off my hands over the sink. Pour some more coffee and reach for another slice of bread.

"No, Darwin. I mean, we really need the money," she says. "We're not going to make rent this month."

"For the apartment?" I stop, bread in midair above the toaster. "What's going to happen?"

"Keep your voice down. It's fine. We'll figure it out."

"No, this is not fine. When Dad went away last year, you promised we'd figure it out. That Runt and me wouldn't go stay with Aunt Martha. Or to social services, like the kids down the hall. You promised back then we'd *figure it out*."

"I know, I know," she says, putting her mug on the counter. "And I'll keep that promise. Things are just a little tight."

We stare at each other uneasily. Then I snap.

"It's 'cause you're spending it all on Norfolk. Isn't it?" I take a step closer to her. "You're giving away all the money we need for a roof over our heads. Giving it to a bunch of rich folks in the suburbs so that they can get richer. While we get poorer."

"So you can get a proper education," she hisses. "And not end up on the streets. Or worse, like your daddy."

"Don't say that about Dad."

"He nearly beat a man to death, Darwin."

"Dad decked a guy who deserved it."

"Your father was drunk. And violent. And it was only a matter of time before

40

he brought both of those things home to us."

"Shut up!" I shout.

"Don't you speak to me like that." Her face twists in anger. "You did nothing but get into trouble at school, even before your daddy went to prison. Now don't tell me that I made the wrong call giving everything we have to get you to a better place." She taps me on the chest. "I always put this family first. And now you have to as well. Make something of the chance I'm giving you. Don't you forget it."

I shrug, suddenly helpless. Feeling like someone just pulled my plug, and I'm empty of anger, of everything. I'm tired of it all. Just like Mom is, I guess.

"I'm sorry," I say.

"What's going on?" says Runt, standing in the doorway, hair spiked up from sleep.

"Nothing, honey," says Mom. She wipes her eyes with the palms of her hands. "You want some Cheerios?"

I watch her pour a bowl for him while he waits, spoon in hand. "Keep an eye on him while I shower?" she says. I nod, and she disappears into her room. Runt turns on the TV, switching channels until he gets to cartoons.

"That stuff will rot your brain, Runt," I say, not really thinking about it.

"I know," he says happily, around a mouthful of cereal. I'm watching him eat when I think of something. I go to the bedroom and pull out the bills from the jeans I wore yesterday. The fifty Jonathan gave me. Not much, but rent's due soon. Maybe I can pull together some more by then. And figure out how to lie to Mom about it.

Chapter Eight

We rush to catch the last train out from downtown. Cold, hard stars above the entrance to the subway platform. Nothing on the street except some black-and-white cabs. Meth head holding out his ballcap to us at the top of the stairs. Keisha pushes closer to me as we walk by him. He gives me a rotten-toothed smile. I give him a hard look and he turns away.

I keep my arm around her as we walk down the long tunnel to the eastbound platform. Our steps fall into the same rhythm. Her hair smells nice, a little like peach or something. We hit the platform. No train. Just an old guy in a long black coat, sitting on a bench, coughing into a handkerchief. And a young kid in a puffy, white snow jacket, looking edgy. I look down the dark tunnel. No sign of the subway headlight. I check the kid again, trying to figure out if he's going to be a problem. Subway isn't that safe at night, even with cameras and cops around. Distracted, I don't hear Keisha until she thumps me on the chest.

"I said, you were quiet tonight. Did you have a good time?"

"Yeah," I say. "Your friends are nice." But she's right. I didn't say much at the restaurant. Weird how you can feel alone in a place that crowded. We had been crammed into a booth with a bunch of her friends, mostly girls. I spent the night mainly watching her laughing, talking about stuff I didn't understand with people I didn't know.

"They're actually pretty nice, if you get to know them," she says. "Which you didn't."

"Don't get me wrong—I'm not complaining about your friends."

Her lips purse as she frowns. She's cute when she's mad. I laugh. "All right, all right. I don't have much in common with them. They're just kinda…"

She punches me again in the chest. "Kinda what?"

"Naw, nothing bad. Just different. From me." She starts to turn away, but I pull her close.

"Look, when we met, I thought to myself, There is a girl who's out of my reach. She's going to college, I'm going to work at—I don't know, a convenience store or something. I live at home with my mom in Franklin Estates. You grew up in a nice house away from—" I sweep my hand around at the dirty subway platform. "Away from this, anyway."

"So you think I'm too good for you?" One eyebrow arches up.

"Damn straight you're better than me.. You just don't know it yet." She shakes her head, tries to interrupt. I keep going.

"But I'm not passing up the chance to be with you just because you're making a mistake." Now she laughs, light and nice, like wind chimes. The nervous kid looks over at the sound, then away.

"Know what, Darwin?" she says. "I think I'm pretty happy with my mistake."

There's a roar behind me as the subway finally arrives, and I turn to protect her from the dust and wind. We take the last car and head right to the back, settling into a bank of red plastic seats. My arm goes around her shoulders, feeling like it's in the right place. Like I'm in the right place.

Back row, two in from the left. That's my desk in History, but there's a guy sitting in it. Blond hair, buzzed right down. Blue eyes set in a soft, pale face. Gray blazer, white shirt, blue tie. Just like my uniform. His pen taps in time with the tunes running through his earbuds, until I tug one of them out.

"This." I nod at the desk. "This is mine."

He looks up, and I'm expecting anger, fear and resentment. Instead, his eyes widen and he smiles.

"You're Downtown Dar. I saw you yesterday." He mimes a punch. "Sweet."

"Whatever." I nod my head to one side. "Out of my seat."

"Yeah, sure." He swipes his binder closed and practically jumps out of the seat. "No problem." He hovers over me as I sit down, like we're about to have a conversation. But luckily Mr. Hassel walks in, and my groupie has to find a seat on the other side of the room.

He goes through the roster and then walks up and down the aisles, collecting our essays. He pauses briefly when I add mine to the pile in his arms, scanning the first page. I keep stony calm, trying not to care what he thinks. I worked hard enough on it, that's for sure.

The class goes by pretty quickly. Like I said, History is one of the few classes I can pay attention in. I mean, I especially like the stuff about wars and battles—everybody does. But I like thinking about the way things could have gone too. The way one little moment could have changed everybody's lives— one speech, one bullet. All it would have taken was one thing and we wouldn't be living the way we are now. Something about that really gets me.

At the end of class, Mr. Hassel calls me out of the stream of students heading for the door. He's young for a teacher, and his suits never fit quite right, like he still has to grow into them. He tries too hard, like a lot of new teachers. Tries to be the "cool guy" and drop lots of references to music and TV shows into his lessons. Tries to be our friend.

"Darwin," he says. "We need to talk about a few things, bro." He grabs a stack of papers, gets out from behind his desk and sits down in a front-row student desk. Motions for me to sit down at a desk next to him.

He clears his throat, then says, "Darwin, you're a big guy. A tough guy. And that's great in, like, football or basketball. But in the classroom, you are just one mind among many."

I don't let my expression change, but I'm wondering where the hell this is going.

"I think you're used to getting your way with things. Because you can, right? Like when you kicked Mark out of his seat at the beginning of class today."

"It wasn't a big thing. I didn't even think you saw that," I say and regret it right away.

"I see a lot of things, Darwin," says Mr. Hassel. "And I'll tell you, bro, I don't like what I see. I mean, throwing your weight around like that? You know that we have zero tolerance for that kind of behavior here at Norfolk."

I nod, starting to steam. Why's he making such a big deal about this?

Mr. Hassel continues. "I don't know what it was like at your last school. I heard you were inner city, and I get that there was probably a different…culture there."

"Culture?" I mumble. "It was a public school. Wasn't a different planet." Mr. Hassel has probably never even left the suburbs. Just stayed here teaching rich kids his whole life. Might as well be a different planet.

Mr. Hassel looks unimpressed. "In any case, you need to learn new ways of doing things, okay? I see you pushing around kids like that again, there will be repercussions."

"Whatever. I get it." I shrug. "Can I go now?"

"Not yet," Mr. Hassel says. "There's something else. This paper you just turned in." He lifts my essay off the pile he grabbed from his desk.

"Yeah?"

"I had a quick read of the first few pages. It's quite different from the other work you've turned in since you started here."

Damn straight it's different. I worked harder on this than on anything else I've ever written. But all I say is, "I guess. Thanks."

"Well," he says carefully, "don't thank me yet. What I'm saying is that it's not like your other work. This makes me wonder if it is, in fact, your work."

I pull my head back like he smacked me.

"What?" I say. "You think I copied it from somewhere?"

Mr. Hassel shakes his head. "I'm not accusing you of that right now."

"Right now? But maybe later?"

"But"—Mr. Hassel has to raise his voice to interrupt me—"what I am telling you—warning you—is that I'm going to look at your paper very carefully. And if there has been any plagiarism, I'll find out about it." He taps the paper with his pen a few times. "So if there's anything you'd like to tell me, now is the time."

"Anything I want to tell you?" I repeat. "This is BS. I didn't do anything wrong."

"Like you didn't do anything wrong when you pushed Mark around? You've got to start coming clean, bro."

"I am not your *bro*, understand?" I stand up quickly, the chair clattering to the floor. "And I wrote that essay and worked hard on it."

"Don't get angry with me," he says in a low voice. "Remember the school code, okay?"

"Screw you and screw the school code!" I yell right in his face.

Mr. Hassel goes super pale. I can feel the hum of blood in my ears, and I think about how easy it would be to really scare the crap out of him. Teach *him* a lesson, for a change. Clear his desk, just swipe everything onto the floor. Throw a chair. Throw a punch.

Chapter Nine

The anger feels like a tide rushing forward, like it's carrying me along and I can't stop it. I step close to Mr. Hassel. Close enough that I see his fear.

Then, the tide pulling away just as fast as it came in, I realize something. I'm sick of people being afraid of me. I wanted to impress Mr. Hassel, show him that I actually gave a crap about his course. And I've ended up in the same place I always do.

I take a breath, it hissing through my nose. Then I lift up my hands and step back, surrendering.

"I'm sorry, Mr. Hassel. I lost my temper. I'm really sorry." I pick up my chair and put it back in place.

Mr. Hassel blinks a few times but doesn't move. "Thanks. But we need—" His voice is gravelly and choked. He clears his throat. "We need to see the principal."

The next couple of hours are brutal, my stomach churning the whole time. The worst part is sweating it out waiting in front of the principal's office. But in the end, I get off easy. The principal doesn't call my mom. She puts me on warning, tells me that I'm getting a break because I'm new. And, I guess, because she too thinks I'm from a different culture. Doesn't want to make an example of Norfolk Academy's only inner-city kid. Not yet anyway.

As I walk away from the office back to my next class, I see Jonathan at his locker. He slams it shut and falls into step with me.

"Heard a rumor you took out Mr. Hassel." He mimes a punch.

"Took him out?" I shake my head. "That's all wrong. It was nothing like that."

"Well, you're getting quite the reputation. Which means we're going to have a huge crowd on Friday."

I stop and turn to Jonathan. "I can't afford to get in any more trouble right now."

Jonathan leans over and straightens my tie. "My friend, you cannot afford to miss this fight. I'm thinking you'll make over a hundred and fifty, easy." I push him back.

"Yeah, right," I say. The bell rings, and there's a rush of students toward classroom doors.

"Tell you what," says Jonathan. "I'm so sure of this, I will promise you one-fifty if you fight. Guaranteed. Doesn't matter if you win." He shows me his best salesman smile. "But you will win, won't you?" I think of Mom and the rent. With these two fights alone, I'd have two hundred. Almost a quarter of what we owe for the month. It's something.

"Deal. If it's guaranteed," I say. "But we've got to keep this thing quiet."

"It's the first rule of the club. We don't talk about it." We bump fists and head to different classes. I'm thinking Jonathan won't talk. And I won't. But what about the rest of them?

The sun's coming down in the sky when I get off the bus. Orange light reflects in the windows of Franklin Estates. Big name for four run-down high-rise towers huddling around a bunch of brick townhouses. I cross the muddy quad to get to Dempsey Tower. I pass by TB, sitting outside his house in his beat-up lawn chair.

"Yo, Dar. How you been?" He's wearing his hood up over a Yankees cap. All black, even his baggy jeans. "Long time, man."

I slow down but don't stop.

"Hold up, hold up." He stands from his chair. "You still going to that rich-kid school?" he asks, and takes a pull from his cigarette. It glows, a red dot in the shadows.

"For now."

"That's good, man. That's good. You come up hard, but now you're making something of yourself, right?"

A streetlight flickers on. I can see flecks of snow starting to fall through the air.

"Like that, yeah. Look, TB, I got to get—"

"Yeah, yeah. You got things to do, right? Let me just talk a little business with you." He steps close. TB's face is still shadowed by his cap. "Dar, you're still one of the biggest dudes in the estates. You ever want a job with my crew, I'll give it to you in a minute. " He jabs at the air with his cigarette to make the point.

"A job, huh?"

"Uh-huh," he says, blowing a stream of smoke out the side of his mouth. "You could be my enforcer. Get things done for me. Keep customers in line."

"Let me think about it," I say.

TB takes a final drag, then drops the cigarette to the ground and crushes it with his shoe.

"You do that, Dar. 'Cause I know that you got a bright future right here.

In Franklin Estates, baby!" He swings his arms wide, like he's embracing the run-down tower above him. I nod without meeting his eyes and get moving.

The elevator's broken. Again. I walk up the five floors to our apartment. When I get there, Mom and Runt are out. There's an envelope on the kitchen table for me. Marked *Newhaven Penitentiary*.

Without hesitating, I pick it up and slide a finger under the flap, about to rip it open. Then I stop. Maybe I'll put it away until later. I don't know if I want his voice in my head right now. Just out of frustration with trying to make the decision, I tear the envelope open.

Dear Son, it begins. *I hope you got my last letter as I did not get one back from you. Sometimes the guards take letters and dump them calling it an accident. But really they just want to hurt you—but I fight back when I can. If you get this one let me know as I do look forward to hearing from you. It might be strange but even with six hundred prisoners here I feel alone most of the time...*

Chapter Ten

All morning, my eyes are on the clock.
Last class finishes at 11:50. Ten minutes
to get to the garage before Jonathan
gets things rolling. Eventually, the bell
rings, and there's a screech of chairs
as everyone gets up. I slam my books
and binders into my backpack. I'm out
the door and heading down the hallway
when someone steps in front of me.

"Yo, Dar!" he says. It's the blond kid from History class. Mark. I shoulder past him.

"No, wait, man! I just wanted to say," he says, hustling to keep up with me, "I just wanted to say that I heard you got in trouble with Hassel over me. No hard feelings?"

I shoot him a look as we walk. No hard feelings? I was the one pushing him around. Why is he apologizing to me? The fire doors slam open at the end of the hallway, and we're outside in the cool autumn air. Mark drops back as I pick up speed, jogging down the sidewalk. From behind, I hear him yell.

"You on the way to the fight, right?"

I spin around. Mark stops, panting. Stupid dog smile on his face. Happy to get my attention at last. He says, "I'm going there too."

I stalk back toward him, looking around to see who might have heard.

Luckily, this side of the street is empty, and traffic is pretty loud.

"You don't talk about that stuff, you hear me?" I say, getting right in his face. "Ever."

"Yeah, sure," he says, smile fading a little.

"I ever hear that you snitched on me about the fights, I'll hunt you down." I keep my voice low. There's a mom pushing a stroller coming toward us.

"I understand, okay?" he says. He takes a step back. "You don't need to be so intense about it."

I stare at him a moment longer, then turn around and start heading down the street. A moment later I hear his footsteps and realize he's still following me. Then he's right beside me. It's like having a puppy.

"I could be like you, you know," he says. "I just need to learn some moves."

I look over my shoulder at his skinny face sticking out of the big puffy jacket.

"I don't think so."

"For real! I've been in some fights."

I snort. "You win any of them?" He doesn't say anything. "That's what I thought."

"That's why I watch you," he says. "I want to learn how to win."

"You can't learn this stuff by watching," I say. We round the corner and turn into the alley that leads to the garage. My shoes crackle on broken glass.

"I know—that's just it," he says happily. Like I just proved his point. "That's what I wanted to ask you about." I stop at the door to the garage, hand on the knob.

"Ask what?" I say. "I got to get inside—"

"I want you to teach me," he says quickly. "I want to be your student. Learn everything you know."

I laugh. "You're serious?" Then I see his face. He is.

"Get out," I say. I feel the heat prickling on the back of my neck, the rush of adrenaline. I'm suddenly furious. "Get the hell out of here!"

"Why don't you like me?" he yells. "What did I do to piss you off?"

"It's not what you did. It's who you are." I let go of the door and turn to face him. "You're afraid. That's why people pick on you. It's like sharks smelling blood in the water, only people smell fear. And you stink of it all the time."

Mark's cheeks go from pale white to pink. He turns and half runs down the alley, dodging a spilled-over shopping cart. I screw my eyes shut. What I told him is only partly true.

In a weird way, Mark reminds me of what I used to be. Being afraid like that. Never feeling safe. Growing up scared of the bigger kids in my building.

Scared of my dad when he was in one of his moods. It was my dad who taught me that if you want to survive, you turn the fear into fight.

But I'm realizing that the fear never really goes away. And the fighting only makes me feel better for a moment— the electric shock of my fist connecting with flesh. The drunk power of totally dominating someone. But a second later it's gone, and the fear is back.

I look down the empty alley, littered with garbage from an open Dumpster. Mark doesn't get it. I'm not pissed off at him. I just don't want to watch him make the same decision I did.

I shoulder through the door and into the dark garage.

"Ladies and gentleman, boys and girls. For your entertainment and education, I've found two of the finest fighters Norfolk Academy has to offer." Jonathan spins around slowly under the bare bulb. Enjoying, as always, his moment in the spotlight. Fifty or so students, all in school uniform, shout their approval.

"In this corner, our reigning champion, Downtown Dar Stone!" I don't stare at the crowd, just down at my taped-up hands. The crowd chants, "Downtown Dar! Downtown Dar!"

"And our challenger, Alex the Axe Man Kennedy." I look up and see that Alex is staring right at me. He's got focus. And he's big—about the same size as I am, with broad shoulders. I see Sam just behind him. Looks like Alex is part of the same football crew as Sam. Sam smiles like he knows what I'm in for. I flex my fingers against the tape.

He doesn't know anything.

Chapter Eleven

"Round one, gentlemen," says Jonathan. Alex and I tap fists and then back up. Seconds go by as we just eye each other. Hands up near our cheeks, rocking back and forth. Waiting for someone to make the first move.

"Get into it! Hit him!" someone yells from the crowd.

Like he's following orders, Alex goes for it. A fast right hook. I step back out of the way. He follows with another right. Again I slide out of the way. Edging around the circle, screaming people. Alex has a longer reach than I do. Keeps me at a distance.

Then he changes it up and kicks low. It connects with my left leg, but without any real force behind it. It's enough to throw Alex off-balance though. I lunge forward with a left and then a right to the face. He raises his arm in a block, but I wrap my arms around him in a clinch, locking my fist to my wrist behind his back. An unbreakable bear hug. I shove him back hard.

We break through the crowd. While he's off balance I give another shove, and he smashes back against a concrete wall. His head smacks against the wall with a muffled crack. I keep the pressure on. I've got him pinned.

"Crush him, Alex! Come on!"

Alex pounds against my back with his fists, landing one, then two heavy hits on my kidneys. It hurts, but he's not going anywhere. Or so I think. Somehow, Alex wedges both of his legs against the wall and gets enough leverage to throw me backward. I hit the ground with a yell, more out of surprise than pain.

Lying there, I see him raise one foot over my head. I try to get out of the way as he stomps down. But I'm not fast enough. The boot lands on my shoulder, and I feel a flash of pain through my chest as he grinds it in. I try to sit up, and he gives a straight shot to the side of my head. I see a shower of sparks, and it takes me a second to scramble to my feet. Breathing ragged. Half blind. For the first time since the fight club started, I start to feel a small worm of fear crawling in my gut. This guy has the bloodlust that none of the others had.

This guy wants to see me hurt.

The crowd is chanting. "Axe Man! Axe Man!" We circle each other again, the crowd following us as we move around the garage. Alex sends a flurry of left-right jabs at me, each punctuated by hissing breaths. I weave out of the way. But each time I dance back, I can feel my energy reserves draining away. Much more of this and I'll get tired. Get sloppy. And make a mistake.

I wipe the back of a hand across my bloody eyebrow. I look over at Jonathan, wondering how far he'll let this go. But he's smiling. This is just what he wanted. A big show. Brutal is better.

"Finish him!" he yells.

Fine.

I wait until Alex takes a big swing at my head, a roundhouse. I skip back, just clearing out of the way. As he's recovering from the swing, I kick hard at his left knee. Alex grunts in pain and falls to the cement. Then I'm on top, pinning him to the ground and hitting him hard.

Again and again. Landing punch after punch into his stomach, side, head. Like the piston of an engine, up and down. Alex tries to push himself up from under me, but I won't let him. I'm not thinking for myself anymore. The screams of the crowd become white noise, static filling my head.

Then suddenly the noise empties out. The crowd has stopped shouting.

I'm about to use my elbow, driving it right down into his bloodied and bruised face. Finish him. I look up, only able to see through one eye, the other one puffed completely shut.

Everybody is looking at me, horrified. And that's when I see her in the crowd.

Keisha. Disgusted. Revolted. Scared.

I drop my stare down to Alex. Barely breathing. Red and white bubbles of blood and snot around his crushed face.

I stagger to my feet, feeling like I need to throw up.

"That was more like it," says Jonathan quietly, coming in close to me. He puts a hand on my shoulder. "You put on a good show." Most of the crowd is scattering away through the exits, but Jonathan doesn't look worried. Sam and others from the football crew are kneeling around Alex on the ground. Sam looks over at me. His fat face is streaked with tears.

"What the hell is wrong with you?" he says.

I search for something to say to him. But nothing comes out of my mouth. I just let Jonathan push me toward my school clothes. Let him press the money into my hand.

I don't have an answer for Sam. I don't know what's wrong with me. Outside, in the bright sunlight, I start to run. Not running away from what I just did—too late for that. Not running toward Norfolk, or home, or anywhere.

Just running. Trying not to think. Trying not to be me.

Chapter Twelve

I catch sight of Keisha out of the corner of my eye as I run by. She's sitting in an empty bus shelter, curled up on the bench, arms wrapped around her knees. I step in front of her, then hesitate, not sure what to say. She looks up, and I see her eyes are red from crying.

"Keisha," I say. "It's not like you think. I don't want to do that stuff."

She snaps the words out, like breaking pieces of glass. "Don't bother lying to me."

"My mom—I need the money."

"The money? That's why you nearly killed him?" She uncurls from the bench. "Who are you?"

I can feel some fizz in my blood. Maybe something left over from the fight. Anger. Frustration.

"You're right—you don't know me. And you don't want to make the effort either."

Keisha shakes her head slowly, fresh tears tracking down her cheeks. "I tried, and I think I was fooled by this...this front you put on. You were just trying to be the person I wanted you to be. Someone who is a good man underneath all the tough-guy crap."

"I *am* a good guy." I sit down next to her on the cool metal bench of the bus shelter.

She shrinks away from me. "I don't believe that. Not anymore."

"Don't you even want to know why? Why I have to do this?" I look at my hands, still swollen and cut from the fight.

"It doesn't matter, don't you get it?" she snaps. "There's no 'why' that makes sense of this. Human beings don't do that to each other. Especially for money."

"You know what? People hurt each other every day, every hour. If everybody wants to pay to watch me hurt someone, then so be it. I'll take their money."

"You can't believe that. Some things—" She stops, thinking. "I guess some things shouldn't be bought and sold. I don't think you should have sold yourself like this."

She stands up and walks away down the street, and I watch her disappear into the crowds.

"FINISH HIM!" roars a tinny voice through the TV speaker. Runt jerks at his game controller, rapidly clicking the buttons. On the screen, a cartoon ninja leaps toward a lizard-headed opponent. Despite my best efforts, my lizard man is getting pounded by my little brother's ninja. Might be that my shoulder still aches pretty badly from the fight yesterday. A second later, Runt drops his controller and raises both arms in victory.

"I win!" he shouts. "You lose! You suck!" He leaps across the couch at me. I laugh and let him push me over.

"In a real fight, you wouldn't stand a chance," I say. "You know that, right?"

Runt rolls back and then freezes in a kung fu pose.

"I've got ninja skills," he says. "That's why I win all my fights."

I sit up. "Big talk for a gamer."

"No, fights for real," Runt says, a little swagger in his voice. "At school sometimes."

"The other kids pick on you?" I say. Runt is small for his age. An easy target, I think. But Runt shakes his head.

"Not always. If a kid has something I want, I'll fight him for it."

"What? Runt, man, that's not okay." Runt's face smooths out. Not wanting to reveal anything. He hops off the couch and picks the game controller off the floor.

"Let's just play again, okay?"

I hesitate, then pick up my controller. Runt quickly flashes through some menus on the TV, and then we're back together on the screen. His ninja leaps at my lizard.

"I don't want to hear about you beating someone up, hear me?"

Runt doesn't answer. When I look over, I see the flickering light from the game reflected in his eyes. He shrugs.

"You're a good fighter. I'm getting better at it."

"It's not the same thing, Runt. It's—it's hard to explain, but you've got to fight for the right reasons." The ninja delivers a kick to my lizard, which dissolves in a shower of pixels.

"So what are the right reasons?" says Runt. He doesn't look away from the screen as the words *Round 2* scroll across it. I don't answer. I don't know how to answer. Instead, I just mash the buttons, and my lizard man shuffles toward another beating.

When Mom comes home a little later, it takes her a few minutes to find the envelope with the cash from the fights in it. I left it on her dresser in a plain envelope. It's in her hand when she walks out of the bedroom, holding it out like it's something dangerous. I can feel my heart start thumping, and I try not to look nervous.

"Darwin, where did this come from?"

"Me. I know it's not a lot, but—"

"Not a lot? There's, what, a couple hundred in here? That is a lot of money for you to pull out of thin air."

I feel like crap lying to her. Which makes me even more defensive. "I thought you'd be happy. I guess I should have known better."

"Don't you talk to me like that, Darwin. I have every right to ask where this money comes from."

"It's not like that," I say. I take a breath, trying to cool down. Lay out my cover story calmly. "I've been doing some work around the school. They pay students to help with the gardens, pick up trash."

She grunts and crosses her arms. "Pays pretty well for janitorial. Why didn't I hear about this before?"

"That was just it. I was kind of embarrassed. I know it's not the kind of work you probably want me doing."

"This isn't coming from TB and his crew, is it? Because if I find out this has anything to do with drugs, I swear—"

"Mom!" I say. "It's nothing like that."

"I hope I raised you well enough to know the difference between ends and means."

"What do you mean?"

"That this isn't worth a dime if you had to do something wrong to get it. You need to be able to walk tall and be proud of your actions. Even if you're picking up garbage, you can be proud."

"Right. I get it." I feel like throwing up. I keep telling myself that I'm doing the right thing. Even if it feels really wrong now.

"I hope so," she says. "You should have told me about the job."

I shrug, accepting it. "But the money is going to help?"

"Yes, Darwin. It will help, and I appreciate it. I do. I just worry, you know?" She puts the envelope on the kitchen counter and wraps her arms around me.

An hour later, Mom is reading Runt a bedtime story when the phone rings. I grab it quickly so it doesn't disturb them. Hoping it might be Keisha.

"Yeah?"

"Dar. I'm glad it's you." It's a gravelly voice I recognize instantly, even though I haven't heard it for months.

"Dad."

Chapter Thirteen

It takes me a second, thinking through everything I want to say to him. In the end, I just blurt out small talk.

"They let you make phone calls now?"

He laughs. "Once in a while, if I behave myself. I never called before because—I guess I figured your mother wouldn't want me to."

"That's true," I say. I lower my voice and lean my forehead against the cool cupboards. "So, why you calling now?"

"I wanted to let you know I'm going to be getting out soon."

"Out?" The judge gave him three years for assault. It's been six months. "How?"

"No, not like that. It's just a UTA, a day pass. This Friday. Like I said, I've been behaving myself, and they'll let me out for a couple of hours. I thought maybe I could see you and Riley, stop by the apartment?"

I don't say anything. I can hear Runt and Mom in our bedroom, talking quietly. The click of the lamp turning off.

"I don't think that's a good idea, Dad," I say. "Listen, I gotta go."

"Wait," he says. "Just wait. What if it's just you and me? I can meet you at that park. You know, the fountain? The one I'd take you to when it got really hot?"

Mom emerges from the bedroom, closing the door gently behind her.

I speak quickly and quietly, just wanting to get him off the line. "That sounds good. Tomorrow. Four o'clock?"

"Great. Wait—before you go. Did you get my letters? I haven't had any back and—" I hit the disconnect button and put the phone down. Mom comes around the counter into the kitchen and picks up a cloth to start drying the dishes I just washed.

"Who was that?"

"Nobody. A friend. I'll be home a little late on Friday." She nods, hands me a dish to put away. I wait for the follow up, the interrogation. But she's lost in her own thoughts. Thinking about something else, probably money. I used to get angry when she was like this. Distracted. But right now I'm grateful she's not paying attention—I don't want her to look too hard at me. And that makes me feel ashamed.

The thudding of my gloves into the heavy bag follows a rhythm. One, two, three. Right punch, left, right for the finish. Again. There are other rhythms in the school gym too—the repetitive clank of weights, the ticking of a skipping rope. I like those sounds. They let me focus. One, two, three. Forget about everything. One, two, knockout punch. One, two—

"Downtown Dar!"

Breathing hard, I turn around to see Jonathan smirking at me. He's wearing the sunglasses again, trying to look like a player. Even a Kangol hat this time. Gangster.

"What do you want, Jonathan?"

"Just wanted to check in on you, man."

I turn back to the bag, steady its swaying with one glove, get focus. "What's the problem, Jonathan?"

"No problem," he says. Then he steps closer and lowers his voice. "I just heard that some teachers were asking around. About the last fight."

"Yeah?" I bring up my fists.

"I was worried about Alex and the football crew snitching on us after you laid that beating down. But those guys are worried about getting scholarships to college. Anything comes out about them being involved in the fight club, it might screw up their chances at some big money. They'll stay quiet."

I nod. Pound the bag a couple of times. Heavy hits that rock the bag back and forth.

"So what's the problem?" I say.

"No problem," repeats Jonathan. He moves around to steady the swaying punching bag. Standing behind it, he leans toward me. "In fact, I think we're going to have our biggest crowd ever tomorrow."

"What?" Sweat stings my eyes, and I rub it away with my arm. "What are you talking about?"

"Friday fight club. Tomorrow."

"No, you don't get it. I'm out." I come closer to him, looking around to see if anyone can hear us. "That was my last fight. I could have killed that guy."

"Don't be dramatic," Jonathan snaps. "You tuned him up—he took his chances. He knew your reputation."

"My reputation?" I stare down at my gloves. "I'm not a—"

"A what? A fighter? A killer in the ring?" Jonathan steps in front of the bag. Points at the big mirror on the wall beside me. "Look at yourself. You've got to see yourself the way everybody else in this school sees you. They see dangerous. They see a tough guy from the streets. And you know what? Because of that, every girl wants you. And every guy wants to beat the crap out of you." He puts an arm around my shoulder. I look at the two us in the mirror for a moment.

"You're full of crap, Jonathan."

"Maybe." He laughs. "But that's what I'm good at. I'm a promoter. I'm making you money for just being who you are."

"You don't know anything." I shrug his arm off of me and turn back to the punching bag. "I'm done. Find someone else." I tighten the Velcro on my gloves. Get ready to start up again. But Jonathan puts one hand on my chest and with the other takes off his sunglasses to look me in the eye.

"Dar, let me ask you something. Where do you think you fit in at Norfolk?"

I swat his hand off my chest, but I don't say anything.

"Are you down with the jocks headed for college? You hang out with the sons and daughters of investment bankers? Invite your homies over to the pool at your mansion?"

I snap a hard right punch into the bag, making a deep, muffled thud.

"That's right. You know and I know—everybody knows," Jonathan goes on, "that you don't belong here."

Screw him. Screw them. I unleash a flurry of punches to the bag.

"You only got in as a charity case," Jonathan continues. "You're never going to be on the real inside because everyone knows who you are—an outsider."

The big red bag is rocking back and forth so badly that I miss a punch. I stumble, chest heaving.

"What's your point?" I say.

"My point is, you should go with it. Be the inner-city monster of Norfolk Academy. Downtown Dar."

"You think of me like that?" I say. "You think this is all I am?"

Jonathan slides his sunglasses back on and smiles. "I'll see you tomorrow in the garage. Regular time."

Chapter Fourteen

I walk underneath the big trees of the park. Orange and red leaves above. Brown leaves crunching underfoot. The sharp afternoon air smells like snow. I arrive at the plaza, a round space dominated by a big fountain. In the summer kids splash around in it, but right now it's like a big, empty concrete bowl. I scan the plaza, checking out couples and families on the benches. Two kids kicking a soccer ball. And, on the other side of the fountain, someone hunched over a table. I recognize the black leather jacket. Dad. I'm seized by the urge to turn around and walk away. Not deal with him. With the mess he's made of my family. At the same time, there's a part of me that's a little kid like Runt. That just wants to bring him home. Have a dad again, even if he screwed up.

He looks up when I approach. I can see the years in the wrinkles around his eyes, like I can with Mom. He smiles uncertainly and stands up, not sure if he should hug me or shake hands.

"Man, I think you grew," he says. "Look at you."

I smile and shake my head. "It's only been six months, Dad."

"You say it like six months isn't a long time. Hey, sit—sit down."

I do, on a concrete bench alongside the table. Engraved into the table is a chessboard, the flecked black and white squares embedded in its surface. I've seen old guys playing here on weekends, staring intently at their little pieces.

I study Dad's face for minute. "So how's it been?" I ask.

"I'm holding my own." He leans across the table. "Food's a little better than your mom's, actually." I laugh. "And I've been playing my cards right, behaving good. Already got this 'unescorted temporary absence.' Maybe I'll get more of them. See you some more? Maybe see Riley next time?"

"I don't know about that. I'm not sure if Mom would let that happen."

"Huh," he says. He pushes up the sleeve of his leather jacket to scratch his forearm. There's a new tat there, a small spiderweb. "Well, she let you come today, right?"

I shrug and look away.

"Your mother doesn't know you're here, does she?" I look back sharply, and his brown eyes bore into mine.

"She'd just get mad," I say. "At me. At you."

"Aw, man." He laughs, but like it's sad, not funny. "She's not going to forgive me for a while."

"Forgive you? I wouldn't wait for it. Mom still doesn't—" The words drop away from me.

"Doesn't what?" Dad sits back and crosses his arms, leather quietly creaking.

Love him? Care about him? I think she still does. A long moment goes by while I think.

"She doesn't trust you," I say. "She says that you were always angry and almost always drunk."

Dad takes a deep breath, like he's about to yell. But then he lets it go, a steady hiss of air before he finally speaks.

"Well, she was never on my side. Never understood my reasons. You know, it wasn't always like this. Before those bastards laid me off, it was different. That was hard." He leans forward, tapping the concrete chessboard in front of me to make his point. "And damn straight I was angry. You take a man in the prime of his life and tell him that he's not worth a dollar. Make it so that a man can't take care of his family anymore. I had a right to be angry." He thumps the board again, now with his fist. "That's what your mother never understood."

I've heard this speech before. "I know, Dad."

He looks at me, the circles around his eyes so dark they look bruised. Scared eyes.

"Yeah, you get it," he says. "I guess you're learning about being a man all on your own. Something your mom can't teach you. Doing whatever you need to do to survive. Being a fighter." He flashes a smile at me. Mimes ducking and weaving, throwing a punch. I don't smile back.

"You think that's true? That I have to fight for everything?"

"Damn straight." Dad pounds the table in front of him again. "It's like this game, like chess. It's you against everybody else. You've got to make your moves. Plan your strategy. Never let your guard down."

I look at the chessboard. Black squares marching in ranks against the white squares. "Yeah, that's what I always thought."

Dad leans back, satisfied. Then I continue.

"But now, Dad, I'm starting to think about the game a little differently. See, I thought I was a player. But I'm starting to realize that I'm just one of the pieces. Like the knight or something. Maybe the pawn."

His eyebrows knit together in confusion. "Naw, maybe I didn't explain it to you right. You see, it's—"

"No, Dad. You always explained it just fine. But I think I've figured out the truth. I'm the piece, and I'm letting everybody else tell me what to do. Tell me that there are all these battles I have to fight."

Dad looks at me, searching my face with his dark eyes. "Son, I don't understand."

I stand up. "I'm not going to fight your battles for you anymore. You want to believe that the world is out to get you? That there's no one on your side? Can't trust anyone? Go ahead. But I'm not going to play that way anymore." I stand up and without giving him a chance to answer start walking away. As I walk across the plaza, I hear him call my name once. But I don't turn around.

Chapter Fifteen

Friday morning. The clock in the History classroom is the old kind, with a big white face and black numbers. I can't help watching it as the time creeps closer to noon. To the fight. Part of me wants the hands to speed up and get this over with. Part of me wants the hands to freeze.

"How about an answer from you, Darwin?" Mr. Hassel asks. Damn, he doesn't let anything slip.

"I'm sorry," I say. "Can you repeat the question?"

"That's what I thought." Mr. Hassel sighs. "We're talking about Switzerland being neutral in the World Wars. Chris said he thought they were cowards. You wrote your essay about this, so what do you think?"

He leans against his desk, a little smile on his face. I shrug. His face hardens.

"I'm not giving you an option, Dar. Tell us, what do you think? From all the research you did?"

I look out the window and take a deep breath. He still doesn't believe I wrote that essay.

"I think it's not simple. But they weren't cowards."

"Okay, why not?"

"Well, I think you're a coward if you are afraid of a fight. But that's not what it was, right? They had an army. Like, half a million people, which is pretty good for a tiny country. But they had decided to be neutral way before World War I—like, two hundred years before, right?"

"More like three hundred." Mr. Hassel crosses his arms. "Go on."

"Being neutral was what they believed in. It was who they were. And they weren't going to change that because everyone else was going to war. So I guess I think they weren't cowards. In fact, it was kind of brave."

Mr. Hassel looks at me for a minute, like he's trying to figure out what he's seeing. Then someone else raises a hand, and the class moves on. I try to pay attention but can't stay focused. I keep looking at the clock. Finally, the bell sounds—a flat squeal punctuated by the grating of chairs sliding away from the desks. I'm almost out the door when Mr. Hassel stops me. Other students shove around me.

"That was a good answer, Darwin," he says. "I might have made a mistake before."

"I've made a few as well," I say. "Thanks."

Jonathan was right. The crowd is the largest yet. The empty garage is crammed with bodies. It's a good thing the building is surrounded by an empty lot, or the noise from the crowd would be pretty loud. Inside, it's a solid roar of male voices. Jonathan sees me push between the students and into the ring. He looks like a little kid at Christmas.

"Check it out!" he says. He holds his arms wide. "Look at your fans!"

Yeah, just look at them. Full of adrenaline and stupid. I head over to the broken chair that marks my corner of the ring. As I take off my blazer and unbutton my shirt, I hear Jonathan calling out for silence.

"Welcome back to the Friday fight club! The best in live entertainment! Better than any of that MMA crap on cable!" There are some scattered laughs.

"Today we have a special event for you. A double bill. Two fights for the price of one!"

What? I look questioningly at Jonathan, but he just smiles at me and turns back to the crowd.

"And our first contender is a guest. Someone almost as fierce as our own Downtown Dar. May I present to you... Manslaughter Mason Dillon!" Jonathan points across the ring, and I see a big bald guy emerge from the crowd. Mason. The guy who was roughing up

Jonathan when I first met him. I walk out into the empty space that serves as the ring and grab Jonathan by the shoulder, spinning him around.

"What the hell are you doing?" I say.

Jonathan straightens his sunglasses. "Making some magic. I thought, who better to take you on than someone who has a grudge against you?"

"He doesn't even go to Norfolk."

"What, that's against the rules? Oh, wait. I make the rules. And I say it's fine." The crowd is getting restless. I stare at Mason. He smiles, a flat line under his beady eyes.

"What's the problem?" he yells out. "You afraid?" There's laughter from the crowd. Jonathan turns to me, eyebrows raised. I barely shake my head.

"All right, it's on!" yells Jonathan. The crowd roars like a jet engine.

Chapter Sixteen

Mason's eyes don't leave mine as he shifts his weight, forward and back. Getting ready to pounce. I wait for it.

He comes at me with a right hook. My head flinches back as his fist swings by me, air brushing my face. I snap a right jab in while he's still finding his balance. I feel my knuckles hit flush with his jaw. Solid hit. Feels good. Mason turns and stumbles away.

While he's got his back to me, I yell and charge at him. At the last moment I whirl around and slam his knees with a strong kick. The force of the impact spins him around as he drops to the floor. A good opportunity to get a submission hold on him. But I miss it—I'm too slow—and I'm surprised to see Mason back on his feet. He doesn't waste time, stepping in toward me and lifting a knee into my stomach. I groan and bend over, and he follows through with an uppercut as I go down.

I hit the floor and roll onto my side. There's a sharp needle of pain above one eye. I can feel a warm sheet of blood under my nose. I don't move, because it will make it hurt more. Jonathan comes in from the side, leaning down.

"You finished?" Past him, I see Mason already lifting both hands in victory, the crowd shouting approval.

Not yet. I've got a little more fight. I shake my head and push myself upright. Mason turns around, surprised, as people in the crowd start pointing at me.

Back on my feet, I lift my fists. Then gesture at Mason with one hand—come on, come at me.

He rolls his neck, loosening up. Smirks like this is going to be icing on the cake. Then he runs at me, setting up for a big high kick.

But I step into it, too fast for him. I club his head with my left. Drive straight in with my right fist. Something crunches. Mason staggers back into the crowd, eager hands pushing him back toward me. His shoulders heave up and down as he breathes, his face contorted with rage. He comes at me fast, each step punctuated with a punch.

Right, then left. His speed throws me off. I back up, circling away from him. I move too quickly. Big mistake.

My arms windmill as I try to regain my balance, falling backward. I hit the floor hard, knocking the wind out of me. Mason seizes the opportunity and is on top of me in a second, pinning me down across my middle. He launches hit after hit to my head. I'm too busy trying to protect my face to make any counter moves. My head rocks back and forth from the flurry of blows.

I'm starting to get fuzzy. Starting to lose consciousness. I'm going to black out. I've got to do something.

I grab his wrist with one hand. With my other, I grab his bicep for leverage. Then I push off with my legs, bucking my hips up and rolling over, hard. It works, and Mason topples away from me. We both scramble to our feet, breathing heavily.

This guy is too big, too fast, too strong. A big, angry animal. I can't win on his terms. I need to be smarter. I take deep breaths as I circle around him. I focus on Mason's eyes, watching.

Then I see it—the moment where his rage takes over. A second before he launches himself at me, I see it coming. And that lets me step to one side, sticking out my right arm as he goes by. A clothesline. His own weight and speed work against him as he slams into my forearm.

Mason's feet fly up, and he lands on his back with a solid crunch. I'm on top of him with a sidehold, one leg pinning down his left arm. With my right hand, I lock and twist his left arm up. Mason grunts in pain, but he can't move with me pinning him like this.

"Tap out?" I say, right in his ear.

Chapter Seventeen

Mason squirms, trying to break my hold. So he wants to keep going. I put more torque on his left arm, feeling tendons grind in his shoulder. This time he yells, a thin, nasty scream. I feel a double tap on my thigh from him.

Mason's done. I release him, get to my feet and shuffle back to my "corner." Mason stays down, massaging his shoulder while the crowd roars my name: "Down-town Dar! Down-town Dar!" Eventually, one of Mason's friends helps him out of the circle.

Jonathan comes over and helps me drink from my water bottle. "You ready for the next event?"

"What? What are you talking about?"

Jonathan smiles underneath his expensive sunglasses. "I arranged a little something extra today. It'll be easy for a pro like you." He slaps me gently on the cheek, walking back into the center of the circle.

"Ladies, gentlemen—don't walk away. The main event might be over, but we have a new contender today. Let's give a warm fight-club welcome to Marvelous Mark Ashbury!"

There's a moment of shocked silence, then a wash of laughter from the audience. Mark steps out of the crowd.

He's wearing long shorts, green with yellow stripes down the side. The over-sized fight shorts make his scrawny torso look even tinier. His blond hair, buzzed down to fuzz over his scalp, gleams in the lights. He eyes the crowd nervously, like a rabbit looking for shelter.

I motion for Jonathan to come over to where I'm sitting.

"What's the problem?" Jonathan squats down next to me. He pulls off his stupid sunglasses to look at me, searching my face. "You all right?"

"I'm not fighting him," I say, mumbling through a swollen lip.

"Why not?" Jonathan looks confused. "You're hurt?" Someone in the crowd starts chanting, and soon the room is filled with the sound.

Fight. Fight. Fight.

A thread of blood and snot drops from my broken nose. I wipe it away with the back of my hand. I look across the ring to the other side. Mark is looking down at the floor, smacking one hand into the palm of the other, thin muscles flexing. Trying to psych himself up. I look back at Jonathan.

"That kid is going to get killed. He's not a fighter."

Jonathan snorts. "That's why everyone can't wait to see you pound the crap out of that nerd. Watching you shut him down is why this crowd is paying extra today. Like watching a baby seal take on a shark. It'll be hilarious."

Fight. Fight. Fight.

"I'm not going to hurt him for—" I stumble on the word. Cough. Copper taste on my tongue. "For laughs. I'm not like that."

Jonathan takes my head, his hands on either side of my head. Pulls me close, looks straight in my eyes.

"Yeah, you are. This is who you are, Dar," says Jonathan. "This is what you're good at. You are the monster. You are the thing that everyone is afraid of. That's your gift, man. Now get out there and use it."

He backs up. I rise unsteadily from the chair, and the crowd roars in response. Mark looks up from the floor and scrambles off his stool. I take a deep breath, trying to think straight. Maybe he's right. Maybe I need to teach Mark a lesson. Beat it into him. I walk forward to the center of the ring. Jonathan slaps me encouragingly on the shoulder as I walk past.

Fight. Fight. Fight.

In the center, I stop and let Mark take the last couple of steps toward me. I can see the fear on his face. Jonathan steps close to us

"Ready, gents? Let's do this!" he yells and steps away. Mark raises up his fists, just like I bet he's seen all the guys on TV do it. Like a video-game character.

I raise my fists to eye level. Mark flinches. Sweat shines through his short haircut. But the chanting of the crowd throbs, propelling him forward one step toward me. Then another.

Fight. Fight. Fight.

He takes a weak swing. I catch it with one hand. And hold it.

"No," I say. "Don't do this. We don't need to do this."

Chapter Eighteen

Mark tries to wrestle his hand free from my grip, confused. Jonathan practically runs in from the side of the circle.

"What the hell are you doing?"

"I give up. Mark wins," I say. I let go of Mark, turn and grab Jonathan by his shirt. "And I'm done being the entertainment." I push him loose. As I turn away, I start stripping the tape off my hands. The crowd murmurs, confused.

"Dar, everyone's expecting a fight!" yells Jonathan. "You have to fight!"

"I don't know who I am anymore." I start walking out of the ring. The crowd parts to make way for me, and I stop on the edge. "But I don't fight for you. Or them."

The garage is silent as I leave, the steel door slamming behind me.

Mr. Hassel looks startled when I open the door to his office. I catch a glimpse of myself in the framed mirror behind his desk and understand why. I try to button up my stained white shirt. When I rub a fist under my nose, it comes away with flecks of rust-colored blood.

"I need to talk to the principal," I say. "I need your help."

"What have you done, Darwin?" Mr. Hassel stands up from his desk, offers me some Kleenex from his desk. "Are you hurt?"

"Remember when you said I needed to come clean?" I say. I slump into a chair across from him. "I think you're right. I've got some things to tell you about."

After it's all over, the cops and the principal let me go home with my mom. On my way out of the school, I see a crowd of students watching the police cars in the parking lot. I see Keisha and ask my mom for a minute.

Keisha sees me coming and starts to turn to leave. Then she stops, takes a deep breath and moves toward me instead.

"Dar, what's going on? I've heard things about—" she starts to say, but I cut her off.

"I have to tell you something. I caused a lot of bad stuff to happen. A lot of people got hurt. Including you. I'm sorry. I wanted you to hear that from me." Keisha looks away, but I can see her eyes watering. "I wanted to tell you that now, because I might not have a chance later."

She says quietly, "What's going to happen to you?"

"I'm leaving the school," I say. "For a while. Or maybe for good."

One of her friends calls out from the crowd, and Keisha looks over her shoulder. "I should go."

"Wait. Remember when you said that you didn't know who I was?" She nods. "I didn't know either. But I'm figuring it out. And when I do, maybe you'll give me another chance?"

She lifts one hand up to my cheek, and I feel her cool fingers pressed against it. "I'll do that."

Chapter Nineteen

Dear Dad,

By the time you get this letter, I will know if I'm going to juvie or not. When I told the principal about the fight club, she said that I might get some consideration for coming forward with the details. For helping shut the club down.

I'm still expelled, of course. But I don't know what will happen next. And that's okay.

You told me once that hate was good. That winners hate just a little bit more than everyone else. And that's how they win fights.

You told me once that every day was a fight. That I would have to fight for everything in my life.

I believed you. I think I started to become someone just like you. Who sees the worst in everyone. Who thinks the world is out to get them. Who sees everything as black or white. Win or lose.

And I believed everyone else when they told me the same thing.

I became what you wanted. What everyone wanted. A fighter. Not fighting for anything. Just fighting everything.

But I've learned that you're all wrong. The world isn't like a chess-board. It's filled with a lot more gray than black and white. There's as much love as there is hate. And sometimes, just getting into the fight means you've already lost.

I'm okay with whatever happens next. I'm not going to fight it.

Darwin

Sean Rodman is the child of two anthropologists, who gave him a keen eye for observation and a bad case of wanderlust. His interest in writing for teenagers came out of working at schools around the world. In the Snowy Mountains of Australia, he taught ancient history to future Olympic athletes. Closer to home, he worked with students from over one hundred countries at a nonprofit international school. He currently lives and writes in Victoria, British Columbia. For more information, visit www.srodman.com.